Blurred Expectations

A Redwood Pack Novella

By
CARRIE ANN RYAN

Blurred Expectations copyright © 2013
Carrie Ann Ryan

All rights reserved.

ISBN-13: 978-1-943123-26-1

Cover Art by Charity Hendry

Blurred Expectations

Hannah Jameson has babies on the brain. It seems that her sisters-in-law are expanding their family in the blink of an eye, but Hannah feels left behind. Every time that little test reads negative a little part of her dies and she feels like her Healing powers are failing her. Her mates, Josh and Reed, are doing everything they can to help her deal with their trials and losses, but they too feel like there is nothing they can do.

Just when the lines of what they mean to each other go out of focus, an enemy from Josh's past is back to prove the things that go bump in the night are real and everything they had held dear is now in jeopardy. In order to fight back and find their way, they'll need to put everything on the line before they lose it all.

Author's Note: This is a novella set between books 4 and 5 to give you a taste of Reed, Josh, and Hannah. It is best that you have already immersed yourselves in the Redwood Pack world, however even new readers will enjoy a glimpse of the Redwood's favorite triad.

Dedication

This one goes out to Tonya and fingers. Yes, you know what that means hon. This one's for you and your support!

Acknowledgments

Thank you so much readers for loving Josh, Hannah, and Reed's story in Trinity Bound!! I love you guys for taking a chance on a menage! I knew these three still had another story in them, and here it is.

CHAPTER 1

The solitary pink line mocked Hannah Jamenson as she sat on her bathroom floor, her free arm wrapped around her middle. She blinked away the tears that filled her eyes, though it was beyond pointless. They fell anyway, leaving salty lines down her cheeks. She'd have to clean her face *again* and put on makeup to cover the blotchiness. With practice, she was getting better at hiding the evidence of her tears. Her failure.

Another month, another failure.

She wasn't pregnant.

Again.

Hannah looked down at the offending evidence of her inadequacy then threw it across the room. It hit the wall with a pang that didn't ease the tremors within her. Anger coursed through her veins, and she cursed. Anger at the goddess for not blessing her with a baby of her own. Anger at the other Jamenson women who could have a baby with only a thought and, in her newest sister-in-law, Bay's, case, an afterthought. Anger at herself for not being able to have a child and for disappointing her husbands, *her mates.*

Josh and Reed were the loves of her life, and every time that little plastic stick revealed there would be no baby, she felt as though she'd lost; that she wasn't worthy. Though they never looked down on her for her failure, she could never be sure what they were thinking. Their mating bond didn't allow that.

Hannah slowly unwound from her fetal position, stood and picked up the pregnancy test. She didn't need to show this one to the guys; she hadn't shown the previous two to them either. They would know the moment they looked at her. They always knew.

Reed and Josh knew her in every way possible. They knew her facial expressions, her body movements, her moods—everything. No, she didn't need to show them the stick. They would know the moment she tried to put on her not-so-brave face and said it would be okay.

Because it wouldn't. Not when she was one woman with two men. Of all the Jamenson woman—the wives and mates of the Jamenson brothers—she should have been the pregnant one. She had the best odds, but, apparently, math wasn't in her favor. She wrapped up the stick and stuck it in the bottom of the trash. It wasn't the best hiding place, but it really didn't matter anymore.

Hannah turned to the sink and ran the tap. She scooped some water in her hands to wet her parched throat, and then washed her face again. She gripped the sides of the pedestal sink that Josh had installed for her the month prior and tried to compose herself.

So what if she wasn't pregnant? That didn't mean she

wouldn't *ever* get pregnant. She placed a shaky hand on her stomach and bit her lip. She wanted a baby more than anything, and the fact that the goddess hadn't blessed her with one yet gnawed at her.

Right after their wedding, they'd thought they had a chance. When that chance was lost in a moment of pain and panic, Josh and Reed had held her and tried to console her, all the while feeling the incredible loss.

But, time had passed, and they were ready.

Why wasn't it happening for them?

Hannah finger combed her chestnut corkscrew curls away from her face and let out a deep breath. Some days she just wanted to chop off the long locks that trailed to the middle of her back, but she knew Josh and

Reed loved her hair long and wild.

Anything for her men.

God, she loved them. She'd met the both of them in one of the worst situations possible. She'd been kidnapped from her home and potions store, forced to watch the attackers kill her mother, and then she'd been stuffed in a dark basement and chained to the wall. She'd met Reed there and had fallen for him, even when they both were certain they would die. The Centrals had taken Reed from his home when he sacrificed himself to save his sister-in-law Willow. Though they had been chained just far enough apart that they couldn't touch, Reed's wolf had tried to take care of her, and the Healer within herself had wanted to do the same for him.

Josh had been a human Finder, someone who could close

their eyes and Find anyone in the world once he saw their face. He had only heard her and Reed's names and had been able to find them. Though their mating may have been taboo to some, their triad was strong and held more magic than most—the trinity bond. They had broken the demon, Caym's, connection to his hell and secured some peace for the Redwoods, at least for a little while.

But, there was no peace in her heart. Not when she couldn't get pregnant.

"Goddess, I sound like a whiny brat." She left the bedroom and walked to the kitchen, her body a bundle of nerves. "So what if I can't get pregnant right now? It will happen. I'm healthy; Reed and Josh are healthy. I just need to believe in it."

She poured herself a glass of orange juice and gulped. The

sweet tang coated her tongue, giving her just enough sugar to perk right back up. She leaned against the counter and looked at the home they were slowly making their own. Though Reed had had a wonderful, artist-eclectic home before she and Josh had moved in, it was nice to see the blending of their lives. She had added the splashes of color and then life with a variety of plants. Josh had added comfier furniture and hand-built units. He'd even sanded down the corners and made them beautiful *and* childproof.

That ache settled in her stomach again, and she shook her head. No, she had to stop thinking about that. She needed to move on and keep trying. Even though it ate away a little at her each time, she needed to be strong.

Easier said than done.

Hannah finished the last of her orange juice then cleaned her glass. Just as she was about to get her coat to leave the house, the hair on her arms stood up, and she froze. Something was off, but what? She used her powers that connected her to the earth and reached out to see if anyone was on their property. She could feel the trees, the grass, and other natural things, but nothing out of the ordinary.

Maybe she'd been imagining it.

She rubbed her arms and looked out the window just to be sure. In the past, Caym had been able to come onto their land without hesitation. They'd lost some of their Pack mates through the invasions and it had torn at the Pack as a whole. Hannah still didn't feel completely safe, though ever since Adam's new mate, Bay, had done a blood bond with Edward and Kade, the wards should have been strong enough against Caym. No one outside of the Redwoods was supposed to be able to breach the wards, but Hannah never left that up to Fate. Their enemies had proven, over and over again, that where there was a will, there was a way.

She caught the time on the hall clock and winced. Damn, she was running late. She quickly locked up the house and made her way over to Bay and Adam's home. She'd promised Bay that she'd come over to help the other woman out with Micah, the newest edition to the ever-expanding Jamenson clan. She failed to tamp down that little bit of jealousy over Bay's new baby. At some point, there was just too much of it for Hannah to bury it all.

"Hannah, you're here," Bay said as she opened the door, her

red curls falling around her face in disarray. Though Hannah had soft curves that her men said were sexy and sweet, Bay's curves were all sex. No wonder Adam had wanted her the moment he saw her—and not just because of their mating instinct. Well, at least his body had wanted her from the start, but that was a different story. With the rest of the Jamenson women being slender, Hannah liked the fact that Bay was similar to her.

Even a witch with two mates sometimes needed a boost in self-confidence. Especially with how things were going lately.

No, she had to stop thinking about that. All it was doing was making her more depressed.

She pasted on a smile and hugged Bay as she entered her home. "Hi, hon. Sorry I'm late. I got distracted."

Bay looked her over and gave a sad smile. Damn, she couldn't hide anything from this family. They all knew.

Luckily, Bay didn't say anything and led Hannah to the living room. Hannah loved the way Bay had slowly added photos to the walls of the house, something that had been lacking in Adam's home before he'd met Bay. There was also a small photo of Anna, Adam's first mate, framed on the mantel. Hannah didn't know if she could have lived with that, but it had been Bay's decision to remember the other woman in Adam's life, something that just showed how much Adam and Bay needed and loved each other.

"I'm glad you're here though," Bay said as she sat down, her hands wringing together in nervousness.

"What's wrong?" Hannah asked as she took a cookie from the plate on the table. It crumbled in her mouth in buttery goodness, and Hannah moaned. "Willow's?"

Bay laughed. "Of course it's hers. You know I can't bake. Thank God Jasper married a woman who can because between you, Mel, and me, we're a bit scary."

"Hey, all of us can bake, just not to the artistic degree Willow can. Plus, why should we when Willow bakes so oh-my-goddess good?"

"True," Bay said as she bit into her cookie.

"But, what's wrong, Bay?"

"What?" The other woman shook her head. "Oh, sorry. I'm just worried about Adam."

Hannah held the other woman's hand and gave it a squeeze. "He'll be okay."

"I know. I *know*. It's just that he's having a tough time with his new prosthesis, and I'm afraid he's doing too much too soon."

Adam had lost his leg in the most recent battle with Caym. Though werewolves were fast healers, they couldn't regrow limbs.

"He's a Jamenson. Of *course* he's pushing himself, but he'll be okay. He's with Josh, and he won't let Adam do anything crazy."

Bay nodded and visibly relaxed a bit. "I forgot Josh was with him. That's good. I know Adam is the Enforcer, and Josh is one of the men who works for him, but, right now, I'm glad that Josh is taking more of the leadership role while Adam is figuring things out."

"Josh will be there for Adam, no matter what."

"Your mate is good like that. How is he doing by the way?" Bay asked, her eyes darkening.

Hannah swallowed the now-dry cookie and gave a sad smile. "He's better, though his voice will probably always be damaged."

Bay nodded then squeezed Hannah's hand. Josh had almost been killed when Caym had come into the den and slit his throat. He'd also crushed every bone in Mel and Kade's son's body. Finn was recovering and was almost back to normal, though he didn't laugh as much, while Josh remained himself, though he now had a jagged scar on his throat and a raspy, deep voice.

They'd come so close to losing them both. Hannah still had nightmares that her magic hadn't been enough to Heal them. As it was, she'd almost depleted her resources and magic in order to do it, and had lost something just as precious. A sharp pain flashed through her, and she closed her eyes, trying to keep it all in. She had to remember this pain so she'd never let herself drain her powers like that again. She couldn't go through that.

"Hey, I'm sorry for bringing it up," Bay said, clearing her throat. "Let's talk about something happy."

Hannah's eyes filled, and she blinked the tears away. "What would that be?"

Bay chuckled and cleaned up the cookies. "You're right. It has been a bit depressing around here. We'll have to fix that somehow."

Micah cried through the baby monitor, and Bay hopped up from the couch and made her way to the nursery. Hannah took a steading breath and followed. She could do this. Just because she didn't have a baby didn't mean others weren't allowed to have them. She wasn't that selfish, even though at the low times she desperately wanted to be.

Where once the nursery had been a tomb and dark tribute to a lost child, now it was a bright room filled with love, toys, and bumblebees. Bay had made it perfect for her and Adam's son.

"Hey, you," Bay whispered as she picked up a bright-eyed Micah. "What's all the fuss?"

Micah looked over Bay's shoulder toward Hannah and held his little fists out to her. She held back a sob of her own and forced a smile.

"Hey, buddy," she said, surprised her voice was so calm.

Bay gave Hannah a quick glance then covered it up with a smile before handing Micah over.

"It's fine, Bay. I'll be fine," Hannah whispered as she held Micah close to her chest. His heavy weight made her want to squeeze and hold him forever. He really was one of the cutest babies ever.

"I worry, but I can't help it."

Hannah shrugged then kissed the top of Micah's head. "Go do what you need to do around the house. I'll take care of him. That's what I'm here for."

Bay looked torn for a moment but must have seen the resolve on Hannah's face. Though Bay could have asked any of the other Jamensons, or any other Pack member for that matter, to help out, Hannah had offered because she hadn't wanted to shut the world away. She had to get over herself and be the aunt she knew she could be.

With Adam's injury, Bay had been swamped with helping out both her mate and her baby. Though Adam did as much as he could, it wasn't easy. Plus, Bay was a strong wolf in her own right and lead the other enforcer's by her mate's side. Her sister-in-law left to do laundry and clean while Hannah sat in the rocking chair and looked down at the baby in her arms.

Micah stared up at her with his too-wise eyes and smiled. Though she knew it most likely had to be gas, a little part of her melted.

Oh, yeah, this kid was a Jamenson.

Any of the Jamenson men could bring a woman to her knees, just by smiling or showing off those green eyes. Though Jasper and Willow's daughter, Brie, was a gorgeous baby that brought those strong men down to their knees as well. Jasper was going to have to lock that girl up when she was ready to date.

Hannah smiled at the thought.

A couple hours later, Hannah said her goodbyes and made her way home. Seeing Micah had made the ache grow just that much more, but his happy face had made her feel at least a little bit better.

The smell of roasted chicken hit her as soon as she walked in the house. Oh, her Josh could cook like a dream. Not only was he a sexy, ex-military, part-demon man, but he was her mate.

Hers.

"Hello, my witch," Josh said as he enveloped her in his arms. She sank into him and drank in his just-Josh scent—that sweet woodsy scent that made her want to purr. His demon-tattooed arms, already wrapped around her, tightened, and she kissed his chest. She pulled back to look at him and his red-rimmed blue eyes looked down at her, searching.

"Hey," she whispered.

He tipped her head back and kissed her. Soft, warmth, love...everything. He pulled back and looked into her eyes while tucking a curl behind her ear. "How was it?"

She bit her lip, and her body shook. "Okay," she said, her voice hoarse.

His eyes filled with tears, and she kissed his chin. That this man would break down with her...

Just...yeah.

"What's going on?" Reed asked as he walked toward them.

She immediately went to his arms and sank into his hold. He wasn't as big as Josh but big enough to make her feel small, wanted. His sandy-blond hair was long enough to brush his shoulders now, and she loved it.

"Nothing," she lied.

He looked down at her with his jade-green eyes, and she gave a wobbly smile.

"Damn, baby. It was negative, wasn't it?"

She didn't have to say anything, but Josh came up behind her and wrapped his arms around the both of them. She stood there between her two mates and tried to be okay with the fact that it might be only them from now on—no babies.

She could do that.

Maybe.

"I made dinner," Josh whispered after they stood there for who knows how long.

"Okay," she said, not that hungry. But she had to eat to stay healthy and to act normal. At least acting it would hide the pain for a little longer.

They ate in a sad silence, the loss of something they hadn't had filling the air. They left the dishes in the sink, went to the bedroom, and stripped down. Without words, they got into bed and held each other.

Hannah lay between both of her men, their mating bond flaring in pain and solidarity.

It would be okay. They had more important things to worry about in their war with the Centrals. Everything would move on, grow. They would live. They had to.

CHAPTER 2

Reed Jamenson added a touch of green to his palette and blended the colors together. With a few more brush strokes, he added leaves to the background of their house. Well, the painting of their home, at least. Hannah wanted a framed painting of their home to be placed on their mantel. Why, he had no idea, but he'd do whatever he could to make his mate happy.

He set down his brush and closed his eyes. God, he missed the happiness in her eyes and the brightness of her smile. Though she tried to hide it, he knew she was breaking inside. He and Josh were right along with her. He hated the fact that he couldn't get his mate pregnant. Kade, Jasper, and Adam had given their mates babies so quickly, some without a second thought. Yet, he and Josh couldn't do it.

He cleaned his brushes then closed the door to his studio, not wanting to paint. Odd for him since it was his passion. Lately though, he couldn't come up with a desire to do it. He could only try to hold onto the threads that were keeping their mating together. No, he didn't think Hannah would leave them, but he was failing her. He couldn't give her the option to leave. No, she had to feel needed. She *was* needed.

"Reed?" Josh called as he stepped through the front door.

"Hey," Reed called back as he took out two beers from the fridge. He used the opener to take off both the tops and walked out to see Josh standing in the middle of the living room, his hands on his hips.

Reed stopped and raked his gaze over Josh's muscular body. Josh was wider and taller than he was, but it was all muscle. Sexy, firm muscle. Josh's brown hair was a bit longer than it had been when they'd met. The man had finally lost the need to look pure military and had let it grow out. The spiraled tattoos that marred his arms were a symbol of what he'd become. His mate was now part demon because Caym had bitten him, but he was stronger than any of them had known, physically and deep within.

"What's wrong, Reed? Not that I don't like you checking me out, but you look like you're depressed. It's the middle of the day, and you're not in your studio. What's going on?"

Reed handed him the beer and wrapped an arm around Josh's waist. Josh brought him in for a hug and kissed him softly on the mouth. Reed had always been bisexual, but never in his wildest dreams had he imagined himself in a mating with two people. He loved it.

Josh pulled back, and Reed took a swig of his beer, the cold brew sliding down his throat. Reed tugged on Josh's hands, and they went to the couch and sank into the cushions.

"I'm just out of sorts. I feel like we're losing Hannah by not being enough for her," Reed said as he laid his head on Josh's shoulder.

Josh rested his head on the back of the couch and wrapped his arm around Reed. "We haven't been trying that long; it'll happen for us."

"But, we already lost the baby before," he whispered, his voice cracking, along with his heart.

Josh kissed Reed's forehead then snuggled closer. "I know, my wolf. I don't know what to say other than we'll be okay. We just need to focus on other things."

"I don't think Hannah is going to want to hear that."

"I don't think she has a choice, Reed. No matter what happens, we have a bond that's going to last longer than anything else we go through. We're strong; we have to be. We've *had* to be. I know she's hurting, but we're all hurting. We're going to have think of the good things that we can have. When was the last time you heard her giggle?"

Reed drank the last of his beer, trying to think of her laugh, then shook his head. "I don't remember. That's the problem."

"Okay, let's make her smile."

"And how do you plan on doing that?"

"Well..."

Reed threw his head back and laughed, a warmth slicing through the cold that had lodged itself in his heart. "Of course that's what you would be thinking."

"I'm with Josh on this one," his wolf said.

Reed laughed with his wolf and rolled his eyes. "I like that idea, so does my wolf, but we're also going to have to show her that we'll be okay without having sex every minute of every hour."

"That does sound like a fun thing to do."

Josh grinned and Reed rolled his eyes.

"True, but it's not the only thing. With this war with the Centrals, we've been so focused on protecting the ones we love that we haven't been cherishing her. Plus the fact that we're trying to have a baby at the same time makes it feel as if we're scheduling our love. Sex is going to become a chore if we don't make a plan to stop that."

Josh ran a hand over his face then scratched the scar on his neck that still gave Reed nightmares. "I wouldn't have thought that sex could be a chore, but with the emotions running through us every time we try, it hurts. I just don't want to fail her again, Reed. Do you think it's because of the demon? I mean, the reason we can't have a baby." Josh turned to Reed, and Reed saw his lover's eyes filling.

"No, I don't. I mean Caym and Bay have both had children. So I don't think it's the demon blood running through your veins."

Josh leaned forward and kissed Reed softly. "And it's not because you don't think you're alpha enough?"

Reed jerked, surprised. "How the hell did you know I was thinking that?"

Josh traced a finger down Reed's jaw, sending shivers through both of them. "Because I know you. I know you think you aren't as tough stuff as your brothers, but you're wrong. You just don't have the same temperament they do. Not everyone can have children right away, some not even at all, but no matter what, we need to stick together. We need to get Hannah to smile again."

"Yes, we do. Though I have no idea how we're going to do that."

"Just be yourself. I mean, you make me smile," Josh said then ducked his head and blushed.

"Aww, I love it when you're all cute like that."

"Oh, shut up."

Josh had never kissed a man before meeting Reed, and Reed knew that Josh was still uncomfortable at showing some of his feelings.

"Luckily, you're good in the sack, or I would take offense at that attitude."

"Good?" Josh growled. "Good is all you can come up with?"

He gripped the back of Reed's head and pulled him close for a bruising kiss. Teeth clashed, tongues melted, and Reed moaned. Josh ran his hand down Reed's chest, and Reed moved toward him. Reed bit Josh's lip and sucked on the wound.

"I love you," Josh whispered into his mouth then cupped Reed's jean-clad cock.

"Fuck. I love you, too."

Reed positioned himself so he was leaning back, and Josh covered Reed's body, rubbing their cocks together as he did it.

"What time does Hannah come home?" Josh asked as he ran his hands underneath Reed's shirt. The touch of those calloused fingers against his skin sent shivers through his body.

"She said she'd be at North's for another hour or so."

"That means I get you all to myself on our favorite couch?" Josh lifted Reed up slightly so he could take off his shirt while Reed did the same to Josh.

With a moan, Josh kissed a trail down Reed's throat and

chest, paying extra attention to his nipples.

"God, I take it back. You're better than good," Reed rasped out as Josh licked the happy trail that ran beneath the edge of his jeans.

"Well, I better make sure you know that. Just in case." Josh nipped the skin right where Reed's jeans met his body, and Reed groaned.

Fuck, he loved this man.

His wolf growled softly, nudging its head along Reed's skin, wanting, needing.

Apparently, the wolf loved this man, too.

Good.

The sound of Josh sliding down Reed's zipper echoed in the living room, and Reed winced.

"Fuck, be careful of my dick."

Josh gave a rusty laugh and slowly slid Reed's pants down so they rested right below his ass.

He took Reed's cock and squeezed it tightly, causing Reed to close his eyes.

"I'm always careful of your dick, wolf boy. But next time you might want to wear fucking boxers or something because I'm pretty sure I can see teeth marks on your cock."

"That's because I'm always hard around you and Hannah. I'd rather see your teeth marks," Reed teased.

"Smooth, and that can be arranged." Josh lowered his body and licked the seam at the head of Reed's cock. Reed could feel the tip of his lover's tongue teasing, playing.

"Damn, you're good at that."

Josh let go of Reed's cock and smiled. "I had a good teacher."

Then Josh sucked Reed whole, the head of his cock touching the back of Josh's throat. Reed buckled and tangled his fingers in Josh's hair. The other man groaned when Reed pulled slightly and sucked harder.

It was the middle of the afternoon, and his mate and lover was sucking him off in the living room. Damn, he had a good life.

Josh licked, sucked, and squeezed until the warm sensation in the center of Reed's stomach wrapped around his back and climbed down his spine, and he came. He thrust in and out of Josh's mouth as Josh licked every ounce of his seed.

"You still taste as good as anything I've had, baby," Josh said as he smiled like a cat with a bowlful of cream.

"Okay, fine, you're fantastic. Good isn't even close for you; you're fucking amazing."

Josh leaned over and kissed him. "Damn straight."

Reed ran a hand against Josh's straining erection and grinned. "Can I help with that?"

Josh smiled and shook his head. "Hannah will be home soon. Let's make her help."

Reed groaned and kissed his mate. "And make her smile?"

"And make her believe we can do anything."

****

Josh Jamenson groaned and shifted his cock in his jeans, closing his eyes. Fuck, he should have let Reed touch him so he could have come, but he'd wanted Hannah to be there. Damn him and his weakness for that curly-haired woman. Now, because he wanted it to be the three of them, his balls were fucking blue, and his cock was about to peak over his waistband.

All he needed was to grind against Reed's sweet ass for a second or two and he'd come on the spot. But then the sweet agony of waiting for his little witch might be worth it. Okay, fine, it was always worth it, but that was beside the point. He wanted her to be there, naked, ready, his. Yeah, he'd wait for her. He wanted to. He had to.

The front door opened, and their mating bond flared, full of life, connection, peace, and a little doubt. It was that doubt they had to rip away tonight. It had started as a seedling when the first test had come back negative and had grown with each month of restless energy. He and Reed had to show Hannah that they loved her and that they could survive, even if they couldn't get pregnant right away. Because, right now, the lack of child was just a festering wound that threatened to take hold and swallow them all. He loved his two mates with every breath he had in him, and he would show Hannah that tonight. Though it might seem crass to some to use sex as a way to connect, they were of nature. Reed was a werewolf, a shifter who was an animal at the most heightened of times. His Hannah was a witch, in tune with the earth and its energy. And he was a demon, or at least a partial one, and had the energy to match. Even though the little things he'd done to show her had been enough for him, tonight he'd use their bodies to show what they meant to each other.

They loved each other. They needed each other. They would get past this. They were the triad of the Redwood Pack, the strongest of the strong, and held the trinity bond. They would be okay. They had defeated a demon in battle and had taken a step toward victory in war; they could handle this.

"Hey, boys," Hannah said as she came in the house. Her ample hips swayed as she took off her jacket. Her beyond sexy walk was an effortless movement, one she didn't even have to think about. Josh loved the fact that she radiated sex toward him and Reed without even trying. Reed immediately wrapped his arms around her, and she sank into him.

Josh came around the other side of them and welcomed her. Her sweet honey and bitter-apple scent invaded his nostrils, and he shuddered in anticipation.

"Hello, my witch," he whispered as she wiggled against his cock. He pulled back so he didn't bend her over the table and fuck her right there. He had plans that included time, teasing, and kissing. Not hardcore fucking.

Okay, maybe a little of that, but it would have to wait. At least like five minutes.

Reed captured their mate's lips and groaned. "I love welcoming you home."

Hannah giggled—yes, they made her do that—and turned her head to kiss Josh. "I love it, too."

She sighed, and Josh picked up on a little sadness with it. They'd been so busy with the war and their own lives, he was afraid they'd neglected their Hannah. He had to fix that. He had to fix a lot of things.

Josh wrapped Hannah's hair around his fist and tugged. The slight gasp she let out went straight to his already aching balls as her eyes widened. He gripped harder, tighter, and her breaths came in shallow pants.

Her pupils dilated so he could barely see the dove gray he loved. The three of them weren't in a dominant and submissive relationship. Though he knew others in the Pack lived that lifestyle, theirs was of equal measure, though he tended to be the roughest. That his Hannah would let herself go in his hold just made him want to fuck her right then.

"Fuck, Josh, look at her," Reed rasped as he ran a finger up and down her jaw, soothing.

Oh, he was looking at her. He was always looking at her. This was the little witch who'd taken him in, loved him when he'd wanted to run, who'd held him when he'd broken. She was his mate. His hurting mate that needed to feel wanted, needed. A job he and Reed could do.

"I'm looking, but I think she has on too many clothes." He

rolled his hips, his erection rubbing against her ass, and she groaned.

"You two are crazy," she rasped out as he scored his teeth down the side of her neck. "I just got home, and I thought we were going to eat."

"Oh, my witch, we're going to eat," Josh said as he sucked the place he'd bit her after the demon fire that had threatened them all. It was a mating mark that only wolves gave, but he'd had to do the same. She was his and through the mark on his neck that ached in remembrance of her touch he knew he was hers, as well.

She buckled against him and let out a sigh. "You're not thinking of dinner, are you?"

"Only if you're my dinner, baby," Reed said then groaned. "God, that's like the cheesiest thing I've ever said."

Josh smiled and kissed his lover softly on the lips over Hannah's head. "Yes, but we love you anyway." It felt so right to have his mates in his arms, loving on them. He'd been the new one in the relationship, the one who hadn't been involved in the supernatural world, who had never felt attracted to another man, yet here he was, in love with both Reed and Hannah and at peace. Or, at least he would be once he was inside them.

Yes, that was good. He needed them. Now.

He rotated his hips so his cock lay in the crease between Hannah's cheeks and moved so he could feel her through his jeans. Hannah sighed and leaned back, her plump ass turning him on more than anything could.

"Let's take this to the bedroom," Josh said. "Because I'm going to bend you over that bed, and I want to lick every sweet inch of your skin so I can make sure I remember what you taste like." And he wanted to make sure his Hannah knew how much he wanted her, but he wasn't going to let her in on that. No, he had to approach that more subtlety. Well, as subtle as he could get thrusting into her tight pussy.

His cock twitched at the thought, and he led both of them to the bedroom, the tattoos on his arms pulsating with each beat of his heart. They'd made love in every room of the house and most of the places surrounding it outside, but he wanted this time to be in the place they slept and let go of their protective walls. They needed to relax, love, and sweat.

Hannah turned toward him and stood on her tiptoes to kiss him softly.

"Get naked," she ordered then bit her lip in that cute way she always did.

He smiled, stripped off his shirt, and then unbuttoned his pants. His already too-hard cock bounced against his body as he released it from the confines of his jeans and boxer briefs. He grinned as Reed licked his lips, his lover's eyes glowing gold with arousal. Josh loved when the wolf came out to play. It was such an integral part of Reed that they needed it there at the surface, adding to the energy of their mating.

Hannah and Reed stood naked in front of him, their bodies flushed with arousal. Without saying anything, Josh knelt in front of Hannah and buried his face in her curls. She let out a sharp gasp as he feasted on her juices. He gripped her ass with his hands and kneaded, and he felt her hand tangle in his hair as she steadied herself. He lifted his gaze slightly to watch Reed lick and nibble her breasts.

Oh, yes, he'd taste those later. He licked and sucked around her clit, her body pulsating beneath his touch. Her taste burst on his tongue, and he growled. He felt the demon within him stir, ready to increase his strength. Though it was still new to him, he had the control to stop it. He increased his speed then plunged two fingers into her pussy. She bucked against him, and he felt her walls tighten around him as she came.

He growled, and his throat ached, bringing him out of the moment. He'd had it slit by the demon not too long ago, and it still hurt. His voice would forever be damaged. He lifted a lip in disgust before schooling his features, but his lovers had noticed.

"Are you okay?" Reed asked.

"Fine," Josh bit out.

Reed leveled a gaze at him then kissed him slowly, licking Hannah's juices off his lips. "Sweet. I love her taste."

Josh let out a breath as they dropped the too-sensitive subject.

"Make love to me," Hannah said.

"I want you to swallow me, Hannah, while Josh fucks you," Reed said as he placed their mate on the bed and positioned his cock near her lips. Damn, he loved when Reed went all alpha. They'd made love in every position possible, yet each time it seemed new to him.

Hannah shuddered at Reed's words, and Josh knelt between her legs, the head of his cock rubbing against her swollen lower lips. He rocked forward a bit, the head dipping into her pussy slightly, and he groaned. Fuck, he wasn't going to last long, not with how tight she was.

Hannah smiled then licked and sucked Reed, slurping and humming happy noises while she did so. Damn, they were lucky men. Josh ran his hands up and down her thighs then slowly entered her, one inch at a time. She was small, and he was thick, but he'd fit; he always did. He rocked into her until he was balls-deep, surrounded by her swollen heat.

Fuck, it was paradise. No, it had to be better than that. He wasn't eloquent with words—he never was—but there had to be a word for that. He pulled out, and she bucked against him before he thrust back in hard. She screamed against Reed's cock, but he continued on. There was pleasure in her eyes, not pain, so he knew she liked it. He ran his thumb over her clit in small circles, needing her to come again because he wasn't going to last. Not with the sight of Hannah's lips around Reed's cock and not with his own cock surrounded by her swollen walls. He flicked her clit again, and she came, hard. Reed thrust again then held her head toward him, his cock clearly throbbing in her mouth as he came. Josh followed at the sight, his balls tightening, his seed filling her.

He pulled out of her slowly then flipped her over. She squealed and looked over her shoulder.

He raised a brow and smiled. "Oh, you thought we were done with you?"

Reed laughed then switched places with him. "Oh, no, baby, it's time that I felt this pussy and you taste our Josh's cock. What do you say?"

"I love you two. You always know what to do to bring me back."

Josh ran a finger down her jaw. Oh, they weren't done yet, not by a long shot, but they were getting to that path. Reed and Josh moved in unison and brought their mate with them. They were the triad, and no matter what, they had to get through this. Sex was a start, making love was the beginning, but there had to be something more for them as well. It would come, soon.

CHAPTER 3

Hannah stretched her muscles after sitting in her yoga pose for too long. She'd gotten distracted instead of trying to settle herself down. She grinned at herself. Okay, her body may have been sore from the thorough lovemaking the night before, but that was another story altogether.

She blushed at the thought of both of her mates' hands on her in every way possible. She knew they had been trying to make sure she knew that they were connected body and soul, and it had worked, at least for a few moments. She'd forgotten the stress of their inability to conceive, the stress of the war, the stress of all the turmoil in their own family. But then, once the warmth and glow had started to recede, the nightmares came back.

She hated herself for being weak. Why was it that she couldn't just let go and let things happen? No, she had to try to force things, stressing herself out even more. She knew that stress didn't lead to pregnancy in most cases.

Yet, no matter how hard she tried to relax, she did just the opposite. Her body was as tight as a coil ready to spring. And, worse yet, she was bringing down her mates too. Reed and Josh tried so hard, yet she felt that she was nothing.

She stood up, stretched her back again, and walked out to her porch. She wrapped her arms around herself as the chilling November wind tried to seep into her bones. She closed her eyes and remembered the previous November. Everything had changed when the Centrals had taken her, and yet she felt she was standing in place, not able to move forward when her body was failing her.

"Hannah?" Reed's voice drifted along the wind, and she stared out into the opening of trees as her mate walked toward her. His sandy blond hair was a little too long, his green eyes bright with tension, his body taut. Oh, but how she loved that lean body of his. He wasn't as big as his brothers or Josh, but he was hers.

He loped toward her, and she sank into his embrace. "How was your run?" He had gone on a run of four paws, rather than two feet. Though, from the look in his eyes, he hadn't released any of the added tension that she'd created and put on him.

"Short, but good." He kissed her temple then ran his lips to her jaw before taking hers in a kiss. "What are you doing out here in the cold?"

She leaned into his body, the heat radiating from him blocking out any cold that could encroach on her. "Just thinking. I finished my yoga, and I was going to go plant something or check my herbs in the greenhouse you and Josh built for me, but I was just taking a moment to breathe in the fresh air first."

He looked down at her, his eyes imploring, cautious, and she held back a wince. She was the one doing this, the one causing the unease in their relationship, their bond. She had to fix it, but she didn't know how.

"Do you want me to help you?" he asked, his voice full of longing.

She shook her head, unable to face him knowing she was the one who'd caused everything. "No, I'll be okay. I guess I just need some time alone."

Hurt crossed his features before he schooled them. He nodded, his jaw tight. "I guess I'll go to my studio. Josh should be home soon from Adam's. He said he was going to make dinner since he still doesn't trust us boiling water."

That brought a small smile to her lips, and she noted the triumph in Reed's gaze. Warmth spread through her at the thought of his love, but she still couldn't climb out of her funk.

"I wasn't the one who used the potholder to start a fire." She smiled again, and Reed chuckled softly, the deep tone causing shivers to race down her spine.

"I didn't use it to start the fire per se. I'd just forgotten it was there." He gave her a sheepish smile, and she stood up on her tiptoes to kiss the bottom of his jaw. This was the Reed she loved, and with him, she was the Hannah he loved. She just needed to remember that.

"This is why Josh cooks for us. It's for our own safety." She kissed him softly then pulled him into the house. His hand was warm and slightly calloused, an artist's hand.

She walked to the small greenhouse that Reed and Josh had built for her and let out a breath. She knew they loved her, and she loved them just as much. Yet this funk of hers was making her feel inadequate. She rolled up her sleeves and dug her hands into the dirt, its nutrients alive and breathing, and her magic thriving. She was connected to the earth in every way possible, and she knew the magic was coming through her, waiting to be let out and be put to good use.

She was so tired of using her magic to protect herself and those she loved. It bordered too much on causing harm. No, she had to be truthful to herself; it *was* causing harm. Maybe that was another reason she felt as though she were sinking in quicksand, unable to get out.

She closed her eyes and let her magic work, the herbs and plants around her reaching toward her, wanting to be near her magic. Before she knew it, two hours had passed, and she could smell the lasagna in the oven.

Josh was home.

She closed her eyes again and flared their bond, sending her love toward him. She hadn't done that in far too long. She felt the love flare back at her, and she smiled.

Hannah wiped off her hands on her apron then took it off and hung it on a peg that Josh and had installed for her. They were always doing things like that for her, little touches here and there to show her they loved her and wanted to make things easier. She knew that, and she was grateful. She even told them she was. Yet, whatever was going on with her was corroding their bond, and she needed to fix it, though she didn't know how.

When she walked into the kitchen, the warm smell of Italian

cooking filled her nose and the smell of garlic bread made her stomach rumble.

"Hey, baby," Josh said as he walked toward her and ran a finger down her cheek. "You had a little bit of dirt here."

She blushed and ducked her head. "Maybe I should shower before we eat."

Josh leaned down and kissed her lips, his ponderosa-pine scent enveloping her. "I think I like you dirty."

She rolled her eyes and bit his lip. "You're bad, you know that?"

"And you like me for it."

Reed came up from behind her and wrapped his arms around her waist. He nuzzled his nose in her neck, and she shuddered.

"Feel better?"

She nodded, though she didn't feel hundred percent better yet.

They sat down and ate, the basil and garlic bursting on her tongue. Her Josh was an amazing cook. Well, he was amazing to her. They all knew that he wasn't as good of a cook as Pat, Reed's mother, or Willow, their sister-in-law, but he was still amazing.

After they cleaned up the dishes, Josh pulled out three beers, and Reed led them to the living room. She sank into the cushions on the couch while Josh and Reed flanked her. Though sometimes Josh or Reed would sit in the middle because they all loved each other equally, she most especially loved it when she was in the center of her two big, strong men. She really was the luckiest woman alive. She just had to remember that.

The thought of their loss struck her unexpectedly, and she bit her lip in pain. She'd lost the baby, their baby. It had been her fault because she had put too much energy into saving Finn and Josh, and she'd lost it. Tears threatened, but she pulled them back, not wanting to let the boys know, but they did. They always did.

Reed pulled her into his side, and Josh leaned over them both, pulling them into his arms.

"Hannah, you have to tell us what you're thinking," Josh said as he kissed her temple. "We can't help you if we don't know."

Hannah pulled away, aware of the pain she felt flare in their bond. "You know what's bothering me."

Reed tried to hold her hand, but she pulled away, unable to stand his touch when she'd failed them.

"Hannah," Reed said, "I know it hurts, but if we don't talk about it, it's just going to fester. Let us in, Hannah. We need you as much as you need us. Help us."

Hannah shook her head and wrapped her arms around her middle, trying to make herself as small as possible.

Josh held out his hand then must have thought better because he pulled it back. She stared at the long scar on his neck, and the pain of almost losing him flooded back in full force. She'd used so much energy to save him that she'd lost their baby. If only she had been stronger, if only...

"Hannah," Josh said, "we need you. I know that you want a baby—"

Her head came up quickly. "Me? Just me? Do you guys not want one anymore?" Her chest ached, a hollow feeling seeping through her.

Josh stood up quickly and pulled her into his arms. She tried to fight him off, but he was stronger. "I want a baby; I want *our* baby. You have to know that Reed and I want you and our children. But, Hannah, all this stress is killing you. I don't know how to help you but I think maybe we should back off and see what happens."

She felt as if she'd been slapped and pulled away from him. He let her go but only into Reed's arms. She lowered her head as her body shook, unable to reach out and touch either of them.

"Do you feel the same way?" she asked Reed, her voice hollow, tormented

"I feel like we lost something when we lost the baby. Something more than a life we could have had. We're losing you more and more as each month passes, and I don't want to lose you, Hannah. You're our mate, our everything. We need you."

"Do you feel the same way?" she repeated, knowing the answer.

Reed nodded, and she pulled away again, and this time, both men let her. For some reason, even though she had wanted it, it hurt more than she'd thought it would. When had she become this fickle woman?

"Hannah, you're not a failure or whatever it is that's going through your mind." Josh came toward her, but she took a step back. The stark look of pain on his face at her movement opened a chasm in her chest that threatened to swallow her whole.

"I can't get pregnant, Josh. Every other person in our family can get pregnant at the drop of a hat. We're paranormal. We're meant to procreate and have babies."

Reed nodded. "I know, and it'll come. We just need to not

stress about it because the stress is not good for your body."

"Not stress?" She waved her arms around then fisted her hands. "How am I supposed to not stress when I am the Healer of the Redwood Pack and I can't even show others that I'm fertile?"

Josh shook his head and sat down on the edge of the coffee table. "Hannah, did you ever think you're not the issue? What if it's my fault? What if it's the demon blood running through my veins?"

Hannah bit her lip as tears threatened again. She was ruining this, ruining everything. She was pulling away and hurting the ones she loved.

"What about adoption?" Reed asked, his voice very neutral, cautious.

Hannah didn't say anything, but the thought had already been there. There were wolf pups and witch babies who needed homes. Maybe not in their Pack since the Redwoods took care of their own, but in other Packs and with lone wolves and separate covens. She knew it was an option, one that she wanted to do in the future. But she wanted to have a baby, as well. She felt so selfish, so needy at the thought. What was wrong with her?

Josh nodded. "I'd like to explore that option. But, I don't think you're ready for that. It's okay to want a baby of your own. That doesn't make you a horrible person."

"Yes, it does. Why can't I just want any child and be okay with it?"

"Because you're allowed to be selfish every once in a while," Reed said. "Even though I don't even think that it's selfish."

"I don't want to adopt, yet," Hannah said, the tears running down her cheeks. "I think that's something we could do in the future, but I want to prove that my body can't fail me again."

"The stress is killing you, killing us," Josh said, his voice hoarse from the damage to his throat and maybe something else.

"I'm sorry that I'm hurting our bond, but I can't help it. I'm trying to be strong; I am. I need some time alone." Hannah bit her lip and tried not to crumble into a ball as she watched the looks on her mates' faces. She'd torn into them, broken them with that last statement.

Both men looked at her, their faces pale, pained. She walked past them, and they didn't reach out for her. They didn't even try. But that's what she had wanted, right?

She walked out onto the deck and took a deep breath in the cold mountain air. She should have gotten her coat, but she wasn't thinking. She hadn't been thinking much in far too long. She needed to get over herself and move on. How could she do that?

She walked farther, off the deck, and onto the forest floor. The trees reached toward the sky around her, and even in the dark, she could feel their presence. She closed her eyes, letting the magic run through her as she tried to calm down. The hairs on the back of her neck stood up, and she felt something wasn't quite right. In fact, something was very, very wrong.

Before she could open her eyes, a quick, sharp pain struck her neck, and she felt her body weakening. Before she hit the ground, big, strong, hands gripped her none too gently.

"I have you, Hannah," said a voice she didn't recognize.

How did he know her name?

She felt her body being carried away, yet she couldn't hear any sounds. She couldn't hear Josh or Reed. Her body was heavy, lazy. She couldn't open her eyes and couldn't call out to her mates for help. She was helpless, alone.

And it was her fault.

CHAPTER 4

Reed fisted his hands and tried to hold back the scream that threatened to overtake him. He'd let Hannah leave the house, and he hadn't done anything about it. She was standing out there right now, alone, in pain, and he was sitting in the living room on his ass. What the hell was wrong with him?

"I hate that she's in pain," Josh said as he rubbed a hand over his face. "I feel like somehow she can't even look at me, Reed. It's my fault."

The tension still running through his veins from watching Hannah walk out the room made his body shake, but Reed walked over to Josh and cupped his cheek.

"What are you talking about?"

"If I hadn't charged the demon like an idiot, he wouldn't have had the chance to slit my throat and Hannah wouldn't have had to use all her power and strength to Heal me."

Reed's heart broke for his two mates, and he kissed Josh softly on the lips. "You were trying to save Finn; you did something heroic."

Josh gave him a hard look then shook his head. "No, I let the demon inside me take over, and I acted on instinct. I cost us something precious and might've cost us something more. I need to fix this."

"*We* will fix this. I can still feel hurt and pain through the bond, and I'm worried, baby."

"Me too. Let's go outside and hold her in our arms then talk. We can't just leave her out there." Josh kissed his temple then took his hand. Reed gripped tighter and held on for his anchor. Josh was always the strong one, and Reed needed him now more than ever. Hannah needed *them* now more than ever.

They walked out into the chilled air and looked on the porch for their mate. Unease crept up Reed's spine when they couldn't find her right away.

"Hannah?" he called out.

"Maybe she took a walk on the property?" Josh said as he

inhaled a big gulp of air. As a partial demon, Josh's senses were heightened, much like a werewolf's.

Reed let his wolf come to the surface, scratching beneath his skin, as nervousness swept through him. Hannah could have taken a walk on their property, sure, but she still should have been visible to them. With the attacks on their den, even with the added protection of Bay's blood in the wards, Hannah wouldn't have walked deep into the forest without letting them know or without an escort.

She wouldn't have, no matter how much pain radiated through her.

Right?

Reed opened his senses and inhaled her sweet scent. He followed her trail to a copse of trees and growled.

"Where is she?" Josh growled, his tattoos pulsing and his eyes glowing red.

Reed sniffed the air, this time catching a sweet metallic scent mingling with their Hannah's bitter-apple scent.

"Someone else was here," Reed growled as his wolf tried to claw to the surface.

Josh walked into the forest and cursed, then knelt on the ground. Reed came up behind him and placed his shaking palm on Josh's shoulder.

"What is it?"

"A needle," Josh bit out, and Reed almost fell to his knees. No, not this, not again. It couldn't be happening again. They'd almost lost Willow to a sadistic bitch and a needle; they couldn't lose Hannah.

Reed moved past Josh and surveyed the area, taking in every detail, every scent, every change in the environment. Even though, as he did it, his body raged. Pain and anger coursed through him, and fear threatened to claw his stomach. The scent ended at the wards, which the kidnapper must have gone through. How, Reed didn't know, yet. There would be no point in going after Hannah on foot or in his wolf form now because he couldn't follow the scent. They would have to rely on Josh's Finding abilities, however erratic they were.

Whoever had taken her hadn't been of their Pack because Reed didn't recognize the scent. He closed his eyes, letting the foreign scent settle on his tongue, in his skin. He wouldn't forget this. No, he would find the fucker who dared to try and break up his family and gut him.

He might not have been the most alpha of his brothers, but he'd kill any who harmed what was his. He'd vowed it before when Caym had taken Josh, and he vowed it again.

He vaguely heard Josh on his phone with Adam, the Enforcer, Reed's brother, and Josh's boss. Even though Adam was still learning to walk with this prosthesis, his brother would still know what to do and would help them. Which was good because his wolf didn't want anyone but Josh around.

"I don't trust anyone. We need Hannah," his wolf growled.

Reed took a deep breath and tried to soothe his wolf. It would do no good to attack his own family out of pain and anger. Though a brawl would help him focus.

Reed felt an arm come around his waist and leaned into Josh's hold.

"We'll find her," Josh said, his voice deep, cracking.

"We have to," Reed whispered.

They turned back toward the house, Reed's body shaking. When they got there, Jasper and Maddox where already on the porch, their eyes gold and their bodies radiating with tension.

"Adam is on his way," Jasper said as he opened the door to the house and walked in. Reed and Josh followed, with Maddox taking up the rear.

"What did you get out of the scent?" Maddox asked.

"Like a sweet metallic scent," Reed answered and shook his head. "I didn't recognize it, so it's not Pack. And this doesn't feel like a Central move. They shouldn't have been able to breach the wards."

Jasper nodded, his face thoughtful. "Josh, did you recognize the scent?"

Josh looked up with a frown. "I'm not sure."

Reed stiffened then walked over to his mate to run a calming hand down his lover's face. "What do you mean?"

"I haven't always had these senses, so I don't know. The scent wasn't something I've been near since I've changed, but it's almost like a memory. Like I've scented it before... when I was human."

Reed tilted his head. "So you may know this guy?" An irrational anger pulsated through him again, and he forced it down. It wasn't Josh's fault that someone had taken their mate. It wasn't.

"I don't know. I won't know until I see him. But, it's odd, isn't it? That he made it through our wards, and that I may know him?"

Jasper stood up and walked toward them. "We'll find her. We

thought we were safer with Bay's blood, but we were only safer from the Centrals. With the war and our losses, we've forgotten there are other dangers out there for a werewolf, a witch, and a demon."

"Shit," Reed muttered, and Maddox raised a brow. "Why can't we just live in peace? Why is everything a God damn battle or war?"

"Because we're different. We're wolves." Jasper said, and Reed wanted to slug the bastard. Less than ten minutes had passed since Hannah had been taken, and that had still been too long.

Reed looked over at Josh. "When we get out of the wards, can you Find her?"

"I'll try," Josh said as he walked to their weapons closet. Yes, their military mate had a weapons closet. Josh geared up with knives, guns, and other equipment while Reed got the small medical bag that he could attach to his belt in case Hannah was... Yeah, he didn't want to think about that.

"We're going to Find her," Reed said. "We don't know if this is a solitary attack or if the Pack is in danger, so I want you guys to stay behind and make sure the Pack is safe. We'll call if we need you."

Jasper and Maddox blinked at the forcefulness of Reed's order but nodded. Reed might not have a title in the Pack, but Hannah was *his* mate, his and Josh's. They would Find her and bring her home.

****

Hannah opened her eyes and spied a grungy cement wall.

Oh, goddess, not again.
She'd woken up in a cold, cement room before. Though she'd found her Reed and Josh through the ordeal, that didn't make it any more pleasant a memory.

She picked her upper body off up the floor and groaned because the aches in her limbs didn't go away; they intensified. She took a deep breath and looked around, trying to get her bearings.

She'd been kidnapped— again. This really needed to stop happening. Whoever had taken her had been strong enough to carry her pretty far. Her magic had touched him, and she hadn't recognized him as a wolf, witch, or demon. He'd been human. Though he'd smelled...off. Like he was a human, though not entirely, as though he weren't quite himself. She wasn't sure what that meant, but she knew it did not bode well for her.

Whoever had taken her had the power, or whatever it was, to confuse the wards and come on to the Redwood Pack land without being noticed. She shuddered as she thought of who or what could have done that because she was now at his mercy.

The basement wasn't quite the same as the one that held Corbin's torture chamber. There were no manacles, no places for her to be tied down and beaten. Just an empty room with a cage at the other end. She swallowed hard as she looked at the thick, steeled cell. It looked stronger than a normal one.

Hannah closed her eyes for a second, not wanting to think about what that could mean because that wasn't a normal cage, one built by a normal human who knew nothing about the paranormal. No, that was one built for something stronger than her, stronger even than Josh. It was designed to hold a werewolf. Like her Reed. Whoever had taken her knew that such things as werewolves existed. It wouldn't make any sense otherwise. Since they'd known exactly how to take her, then it would stand to reason they knew *what* they were taking.

Why was the cage in the room with her? Did they have Reed as well? Her body shook and her hands fisted, terror trying to suffocate her. When she'd woken up in the basement a year ago, she'd been across from Reed. She didn't want to go through it again. Nor with Josh.

"I see you're awake," a voice said from the now-open doorway.

Hannah started and curled herself into a ball. She couldn't feel the earth around her, so her magic was useless. Again. She hated being weak.

"Who are you?" she asked, surprised at how steady her voice was. She had to remain strong and keep some semblance of control. Josh would Find her if his powers were working, and Reed would be with him. She had to have faith in them, faith in herself.

"Does it really matter who I am?" The man gave a small, creepy smile, and Hannah finally looked at her captor in the waning light.

He was tall, strongly muscled, and had a military-haircut, though she could still see the slight gray to the color. His brown eyes looked hard, unforgiving, and he had scars down his arms, and some on his chest, but she couldn't see a lot because of the shirt he was wearing. Everything about him screamed military.

Had he known Josh? Or was this just a man who wanted something paranormal for experimentation? She'd heard the horror stories of the tests that were done on the supernaturals taken from their homes. Josh himself had been part of an elite crew that had known about supernaturals, though his team hadn't harmed them; they'd merely known of their existence.

"Of course it matters who you are," she finally answered. "Why did you take me? Where am I?"

"Oh, good, all the normal questions the captive asks. You must be getting good at this." He walked over to her, and she bolted upright and lashed out, her fist connecting with his jaw. He grunted in pain, but the glint in his eyes scared her. Before she could breathe, he had his hand around her throat and her body against the wall.

Hannah struggled against his hold, but he slammed her head against the wall again. Her vision blurred, and her head suddenly ached as his fist tightened, restricting her air. He slapped her hard with his other hand, and she felt the ring he wore cut her lip. She clawed at his hands, trying to free herself, but he was stronger than her. Too strong...

"Don't struggle. It only makes me want to hurt you more," he growled. "Why don't you use your strength, or whatever the hell it is you have? You're an abomination. I thought you'd be stronger than this."

He squeezed harder as the darkness threatened to take hold. Before she could fight back, he threw her by the neck against another wall. She slid down to the ground, her muscles not ready to move. Her breaths coming in ragged pants, she tried to take in as much oxygen as possible.

Oh, goddess, he was going to kill her, even though he didn't know what she was. It didn't matter at the moment because she could tell he didn't care what she was as long as she wasn't human. He would kill her for it.

"What are you?" he spat out then kicked her in the ribs. Pain ricocheted through her body as she curled herself into a ball again. Instinctively, she knew to protect her stomach and all her vital organs.

"Who are you?" she asked again, knowing she would probably be kicked again for her attitude. But she would not give up. She would wait for Reed and Josh. Or find a way to get out on her own.

"You think you're so cute? Well, if you're not going to

answer me, I guess I'll have to beat it out of you."

He punched her in the face, and she felt her cheekbone crack. Tears slid down her cheeks as she tried to fight him off, but he kicked again, harder.

"I saw you with Josh and that wolf. You're a whore, living with two men, spreading your legs because you can. It's probably because of whatever the fuck you are. Do all of you just spread your legs for anyone with a cock? Maybe you'll spread your legs for me."

Terror and revulsion warred within her as she reached deep within to her magic. She didn't have much, not with the lack of earth around, but she had enough to get him off her. It had to be enough. She pushed with her magic and arms, kicking out as she did so. She got him in the stomach, and he flew back into the other wall.

"Bitch!"

Woozy and bleeding, she stood up on shaky legs and made it to the door he'd stupidly left open. A hand gripped her hair and flung her back. Hannah hit the ground, hard, her wrist fracturing to break her fall. She bit out a sob and cradled it closer to her. Being a Healer, she could only Heal others, not herself. Her cheek and wrist would have to heal on their own when she made it out of here. *If* she made it out of here.

No, she had to think positively. She could get out, and if not, Reed and Josh would be there. They wouldn't let her stay here, even though she'd left them in the living room for time alone. Another sob racked her body at the thought of never seeing them again, never telling them she loved them and that, no matter what, she'd stand by them.

Purpose gripped her. She'd get out of here. She had to because she needed to see her men. They needed her as much as she needed them. Hannah would make it happen. She would.

She stood again, and the man came at her, fists raised. She hit him with her unbroken hand, and he slapped her again on her broken cheek. This time, the pain didn't hurt as much. That didn't bode well for the rest of her.

"You're a fighter. I like that," he growled then took her by the neck again. She struggled, but it was no use. He threw her into the cage and locked it behind her. "I'm not going to rape you. Don't worry. I don't want to catch anything from you and your whorish ways."

She didn't comment that she was a witch and didn't have those diseases. Or the fact that she wasn't a whore. Whatever she could use to keep her body safe from him she'd take.

"What are you?" he asked again, and she gave in. She hurt too much to fight.

"I'm a witch." No need to tell him she was a rare earth witch who was the Healer of the Redwood Pack. She needed to keep some things close to herself, even if it did no good.

His eyes widened fractionally. She could tell she'd surprised him, though how he didn't make the connection when she'd pushed him off her with magic was beyond her. Maybe he wasn't as smart as he thought. That could be good for her.

"A witch? Good to know. But if you use any magic on me, I'll kill you then your precious mates. I'll make it hurt, too."

"Why are you doing this?"

"Because you're all abominations that we should have killed when the team first found out about you!"

She slid back farther into the cage, trying to get as much distance between them as possible. "So, you're military?"

He nodded, a scowl on his face. "You're pretty smart, for a dead girl."

Hannah gulped but tried not to move at that statement. She just had to keep him talking, and maybe that would be enough time for Josh and Reed to get here. The bars were too strong for her to break, and she had a feeling they'd been made for a wolf, something way stronger than her.

"How did you get into the den?"

He shook his head then sat down in front of the cage, his body drawn and ragged. Good.

"I drank some of Josh's blood to get through your wards."

Her stomach revolted, and she barely resisted the urge to throw up what was left in her stomach.

"What? How?"

He sighed and took a gun from his waistband that she hadn't known he'd had. "I guess I'll tell you the story from the beginning, shall I? I knew Josh from the team. He was my subordinate when he first started, but then he moved up the ranks, too quickly for my taste. Soon we were equals in rank, though the bastard was so much younger."

She nodded, trying to keep him going. She needed to give her men time.

"I knew there was something different about him from the get-go. He was too good at his job and used whatever the fuck was wrong with him to find our targets. It pissed me off that he could use that freakiness to surpass me."

She bit her tongue at the urge to defend her mate. It wouldn't do any good here.

"When we'd found out the werewolves and other freaks were real, Josh didn't bat an eye, like he'd found his own people or some shit. I wanted to take y'all out right there, but no, the higher-ups frowned on stuff like that. They wanted to use you or something, but Josh and the others just let y'all live normally." He snorted. "Or however normal y'all fucking freaks can be."

"You wanted to kill a whole group of people because you think we're different?" she asked before she thought better of it. It wouldn't do good to anger him.

"You don't deserve to live," he spat.

BLURRED EXPECTATIONS

He wasn't so different from Caym, the demon who wanted to take over the world and rule the humans. It didn't matter that one was human and the other from hell. No, it mattered who they were and what they wanted. Hannah didn't think this man would appreciate the irony.

"So, you've kidnapped me for... what? What good will I do?"

"I'm going to use you to prove to the world you're all dangerous. Though I would have preferred using a wolf, a witch will do. Plus, I don't think that bastard Josh, and whatever the fuck the other freak's name is, will leave you alone with me for too long. I figure I'll use all three of you if I have to."

He wanted to show the world that paranormals existed? That would destroy them and maybe even the humans. Humans couldn't take knowing about the existence of others; it would be too much for them. Wars would break out, and people, no matter their species, would be slaughtered.

Did this man not know what he was doing? He was going to risk the death of millions because he had a grudge against Josh, or whatever it was he hated?

"You're crazy."

"And, you're a freak. Get the fuck over it."

"You can't do this. You'll kill millions of people."

"You think I care? You deserve it."

"Why?"

"Because you shouldn't exist. You're nothing. You're just something that needs to die."

"Why are you using me to do it?"

"Because Josh is a traitor. He shouldn't have left his men to shack up with a whore."

She bit her lip and stared at the man who had clearly lost his mind. There was no reasoning with him, no getting through to him. Hannah just had to wait it out and pray Reed and Josh could overtake him.

There had to be a way. It wasn't just about her. No, it was about their people. Their family.

CHAPTER 5

J osh closed his eyes and opened his mind to the Finding, the pain slamming back at him as it hit a wall.

"Fuck, my Finding isn't working," he said as he rubbed his temples, closing his eyes.

He felt Reed's hand on his thigh, soothing him. "You had it right when we got through the wards. We're going in the right direction at least. Just relax and let it come to you."

Josh lifted a lip and growled. "Really? Let it come to me? Fuck, Hannah's out there, and we can't get to her because my fucking demon powers, or whatever the hell they're called, are screwing up my Finding. And, you want me to 'let it come to me'? Jesus."

"Feel better now that you've yelled at me?" Reed asked as he drove down the winding road where Josh had Found the path leading to their mate.

As soon as Reed had proclaimed that he and Josh were going to Find Hannah, they'd geared up and started driving. It had only taken maybe thirty seconds once Josh was beyond the wards of the den for his powers to work. But, now that he was trying to force it, his powers were fading. He fucking hated the demon bite that had screwed up his Finding. He let out a breath. No, without the bite, he wouldn't have had the strength to protect those he loved, so he needed to keep it in perspective. But it was hard as hell to do that when his mate was in a dark basement and bleeding.

Yes, he'd seen that when he'd used his powers and cursed. He'd almost caused Reed to run off the road when he'd seen Hannah's swollen face in his mind because his body had jerked so violently. When his Finding actually worked, he could Find any face he'd seen before and follow that path. But with the demon blood running through his veins, his powers were spotty now, at best.

"We'll find her, Josh," Reed whispered as he took another sharp curve.

Josh nodded even as fear clawed at his belly. "We can still

feel her in the bond, so we know she's alive."

"Yes, and we can use that to find her once we get closer. I know our bond isn't like Adam's and Bay's. They can find each other no matter the distance, but we can find her once we're closer."

Josh let out a curse. "We just have to get there. Meaning my Finding actually has to fucking work."

"It will."

"Who took her, Reed?"

"I don't know, but you said the scent was almost familiar, right?"

Pain ate at him, and he cracked his knuckles. "I think so. That means I knew this guy, Reed. This guy came after our Hannah because of me." The last word cracked when he said it, not because of the damage to his throat, but because he couldn't hold in the emotion anymore. Damn it, he had to be strong for her.

"No, this guy came after Hannah because he's insane or because of something else, but this is *not* your fault."

"We don't know that."

"Fine, but dwelling on it doesn't help your Finding, and it's not helping Hannah. So get over yourself for a minute and Find our mate." Reed's eyes glowed as his voice rose, and Josh reached to squeeze his mate's thigh.

"Thank you."

"Find her."

Josh closed his eyes and summoned his powers, or whatever he did to get them to work. He didn't have a name for it and didn't really want to name it. He was the only one of his kind in existence that he knew of, so it had never seemed important. He opened up is Finding, and this time, instead of hitting a wall, he continued down a fraying path until he saw her.

He let out a breath then cursed.

Fuck, she was in a cage and hurt. Really fucking hurt.

He could see only her and the bars around her, and she was talking, though he couldn't hear what she said. He concentrated, tugging on that fragile bond in his Finding and wrapping it around their trinity bond. He'd never done it before, but he knew it was the thing to do. As it melded, the connection grew stronger, their bond flaring back to life. It sparked, warmed, strengthened.

There.

"Keep going down this road for another mile then take a turn into a copse of trees that looks like a run-off. She's in an abandoned building three miles past that."

Reed growled and sped up. "I knew you could do it."

"She's hurt, Reed."

Josh could hear the strain of the steering wheel under his mate's hands as Reed fought his wolf for control. He was doing his own fighting with his demon.

"Can you see who has her?" Reed asked as he took the turn a little too fast.

Josh braced himself against the door and focused his energy. "I'm looking." He recognized the cage from a military bunker that he thought he'd destroyed and cursed again. Fuck, this was someone from his team. It had to be. He looked around, though it was hard to do because he could really focus on only Hannah, but he tried. There weren't any other noticeable marks around, just the cage and her. When she held her wrist to her chest in pain, he growled...then saw him.

Cyrus Ferns.

His old commander.

Fuck.

"I see him. He's that fucker from my team that was a hot head. He hates paranormals, Reed."

"We'll kill him."

Though Cyrus was a human, and Josh wouldn't have normally killed a man like that, this was different. This man was dangerous. Dangerous to his Pack, his family...his Hannah.

Reed stopped the car and cut the engine about a mile away from the place where Cyrus held Hannah. Josh nodded then rubbed Reed's thigh again.

"We'll go on foot so we have a better chance of getting him," Josh said, and Reed slid a golden glance at him.

"Okay, soldier-man, I got it," he said dryly.

"Sorry, I'm just thinking aloud," he said as he got out of the car and checked his ammo. The need to find Hannah and get the fuck out of there filled him. He wanted to be in his home, his den, and wrap himself around her and never let go.

Soon.

After he took care of this fucking prick.

"Change to your wolf, Reed. We need your senses for traps."

Reed nodded then stripped out of his clothes and put them in the vehicle. Josh glanced at the tanned body that he loved then forced his gaze away to check his surroundings. From this distance, they couldn't see the building, but Josh could feel it there. He couldn't see any surveillance or signs of a trap, and Josh was damn good at spotting those.

After all, it had been his job for most of his life, and now as one of Adam's enforcers, his protection level had increased.

He heard a sharp groan as Reed finished shifting. He knew the change was as brutally painful as it was beautiful in its outcome. The russet-colored wolf came to sit by him, and he rubbed his mate behind the ears. Reed leaned into him as they both surveyed the area with a keen focus.

Reed huffed out a breath and started toward the building.

Good, that meant Reed didn't sense anything out of the ordinary either.

They slowly made their way to the building, making sure they knew where all the exits were and had an escape path if needed. If they were lucky, they could overpower Cyrus and get out of there with Hannah quickly. But, they were never that lucky.

The building was an old storehouse that must have been part of an older dwelling. It had long since fallen into disrepair. Josh knew she was in the basement, and he could also feel that only she and Cyrus were in the area.

Apparently his demon powers were better than he'd thought.

Reed went first and sniffed around then did an awkward nod. Josh nodded back. Good, there wasn't anyone around, and Josh agreed. Josh made his way to the door and gripped his gun tighter.

This was it.

Yet it all seemed so familiar.

He'd found his Reed and Hannah by breaking into an abandoned building when Corbin and Caym had taken them. But now he was different, stronger, and not afraid of the things that could kill him.

Well, not really.

He was afraid only of losing Hannah and Reed. They were his everything.

He quietly opened the door and did a quick glance of the hallway. Empty. Good. He went in first, letting Reed creep behind him, protecting him from anything that could come up from behind. Josh followed their bond until he reached another door farther down the empty hallway.

He knew the basement was through that door as well as he knew Hannah and Cyrus were beyond it. He turned the knob and crept down the stairs, Reed on his tail.

Cyrus stood by the cage where Hannah lay. His old friend's body looked haggard, bruised.

Good, Hannah had gotten some good punches in.

Josh spared a glance for Hannah and noticed her eyes brighten, but other than that, she didn't acknowledge them. Good.

She would have felt them through the bond as they got closer, so they hadn't surprised her to the point she would give away their arrival and location.

"I see you're here, Josh," Cyrus said as he turned around. "You really didn't think you could sneak up on me, did you? I trained you, boy."

"Let her go, and I'll let you die quickly," Josh said as he gripped the gun harder.

Cyrus just shook his head. "You're a fucking traitor and a sick freak. But I'm the one with the gun on your whore."

Reed growled at the word, and Josh bit his tongue. "Put the gun down, Cyrus."

"No, I'm the one with the power. You put *your* fucking gun down."

Josh shrugged. He had another two strapped to him plus his knives, and the fact that he was a partial demon made him faster and stronger than Cyrus. Not to mention that Reed was a werewolf and could rip Cyrus's head from his body with one strong bite. But Josh put the gun down anyway. He didn't want to anger Cyrus any more than the man already was. That would risk causing Hannah more harm. Anything but that.

"Good. Now you see that I'm the one in control. You shouldn't have left your blood with the Navy though Josh. This is all your fault you know."

Josh made a mental note to visit the base and take care of any loose ends that might have been lost. After he killed the bastard in front of him. He'd also have to tell Edward that even though his blood had changed with the demon bite, there was still a way through the wards with his old blood.

"Let Hannah go."

Cyrus threw his head back and laughed. "No, I don't think I will. Things like you and your pussy here need to be put down. Humans are the powerful ones. If we weren't, why are you the ones in hiding and we're free?"

"Because we let you," Josh said and watched as Cyrus growled and tried to pull the trigger.

But, Reed was faster. Before Josh could blink, a red blur bit through Cyrus's wrist, severing his hand and the gun along with it. Cyrus screamed in pain then went silent as Reed snapped his neck. Reed howled as Josh ran to the cage and broke the lock using all of his strength.

Hannah was in his arms in the next instant, her body shaking as he ran his hands down her body, checking for broken bones. The bastard had broken her wrist and cheekbone, but the rest seemed only bruised, except for perhaps a cracked rib or two.

Josh shuddered as he held Hannah close to him, her sweet scent washing over him as he felt Reed change back to his human form.

"Thank you," Josh whispered as a naked Reed wrapped his arms around them.

"I couldn't let you do that to someone you knew," Reed said as he kissed Hannah's temple. "Hannah, baby, we'll take care of you."

"I knew you would," she rasped. "Though I got a few hits in."

Josh picked her up and kissed her softly, aware of her hurts. "We'll take you home and clean you up, baby." He felt Reed reach into his pocket and pull out his phone.

"I'm going to call Adam and tell him to send a cleanup crew then get North to our house to take care of Hannah."

"Let's go home," Josh said as he carried Hannah out of the room, leaving behind the dead man he'd once trusted. That man was his past, but the woman in his arms and the man beside him were his future.

CHAPTER 6

One Month Later
Hannah snuggled between her two men as they shifted in their sleep. Josh's hand was on her breast, kneading even as he rocked against her from behind, while Reed's hand drifted down her belly to rub her softly. She moaned and leaned into Reed then back into Josh, loving

the way they woke up in the morning.

In the month since her attack, she'd healed and let go of the pressure. She'd had to. She and her men made love daily, softly, forcefully, and everywhere in between. But she didn't stress about conceiving. She'd almost lost her life and risked her mates' lives because she'd been so stressed and lost her focus. The lines of what she could do and what mattered had been blurred, and she'd almost lost herself.

But, not anymore.

She felt Josh shift and heard the nightstand drawer open, sending shivers of anticipation down her spine.

"Good morning," Reed said against her lips, and then he kissed her, his tongue tangling with hers. He increased the pressure of his hand, her body opening for him as he curled two fingers within her. She rubbed against him, wanting more.

"Greedy," he whispered.

"I want you," she said, panting.

"You'll have me," Reed said as he picked up the tempo, hitting that spot to send her over. Her body flushed, tingled, and cascaded as she came.

Josh moved her leg, and then she felt the cool lube at her back entrance, his fingers soon following.

"Good morning, baby," Josh said, his voice low, needy.

He worked her slowly while Reed teased her nipples. She closed her eyes, taking in every sensation she could, even though there were too many for her to count, to feel.

Josh moved back, and then she felt the head of his cock pushing in her past that tight ring of muscles. She stiffened at the familiar intrusion, and Reed rubbed her clit to make her relax.

"Take him in, love. Then I'll fill you up," Reed said, and she could feel his cock throb against her mound.

She nodded, unable to speak as Josh filled her.

"Damn, mate of ours, I love filling this ass," Josh said as he stilled, her body slowly relaxing even more.

Reed lifted her leg higher and slowly, oh so slowly, filled her pussy. When he was seated, Hannah moaned, her body too full, too needy.

"I need you to move, or stay still, or I don't know. Do something, anything. Oh, goddess, I love this. I love you," she said as her body shook.

Josh licked and nipped at her neck as Reed rolled her nipples.

Then they moved.

In tandem, they filled her, alternating so she could feel their cocks rub against the soft tissue separating them.

Oh, goddess.

They increased the pace as her body heated, her climax coming...soon. Josh bit down on the mate mark as Reed thrust, hard.

Her body shattered.

She came on a wave, her men following her as they panted and slowed, their bodies pooling in a state of carnal bliss.

"Best wake-up ever," Reed said, breaking the silence. Josh chuckled behind her, but she didn't say anything, merely cuddled deeper into their holds.

"I love you," she said.

"I love you, too," her men said as one.

They lay down together for a bit longer before necessities and time tables forced them up. They had family lunch at Edward and Pat's house and were going to be late if they didn't hurry. She forced herself and her men to shower separately, or they'd never leave, and then she finished getting ready.

They drove to the Alpha's home, a giddy excitement running through her. This was family; she loved it. They were greeted by all of the Jamensons, big and small. The sight of Micah, Finn, and Brie didn't cause that ache anymore.

As they ate, they discussed the upcoming frost, the goings on of the Pack, and the dangers that lurked.

"We need to be aware of all dangers," Edward said as he held his grandson Micah closer to him. "It's not just the Centrals out there, and we need to remember that. But we must also remember what is good." He smiled at

Micah, and Hannah gripped her men's hands as emotion welled over at the picture. "This family is what is good. We'll survive. We always have, and we will continue."

Hannah looked over at North as he patted Ellie's shoulder. A dark look passed over her face. Maddox stood up from the table abruptly and picked up Finn.

"He needs to be changed."

He left the room, and the others looked around, confused.

Their family was changing. With each addition, the dynamics evolved, and Hannah was part of that. She leaned into Reed's side as Josh rubbed her knee.

These were her mates. Her wolf and demon. Hers.

****

"Push, Hannah, push," Josh said as he kissed his mate's brow. She gripped his hand as Reed gripped her other.

Josh looked over at the other man and gulped. Jesus, why did they always say childbirth hurt only the mother? From his perspective, they were both about to pass out.

She'd been pregnant at that lunch with the Jamensons. She'd also been pregnant when Cyrus had taken her, though she'd only just conceived that day, or sometime close to then.

Josh shook his head then kissed Hannah again. Things had a way of coming full circle and scaring the crap out of him.

Here he was, about to be a father, and all he wanted to do was sit down so he didn't faint and look like a pussy. From the look of Reed, Josh figured he wasn't alone.

Thank God.

"Okay, Hannah, you're doing good," North said as he smiled.

Fuck that. Why did that man smile? Shouldn't he be helping to get this done already? Didn't he see Hannah was hurting?

Okay, maybe he needed to back off a bit.

"Push one more time, and we'll have a baby for you to hold," North said as Cailin, Reed and North's sister, stood behind him, ready to help with the newborn. She'd pulled her thick black hair from her face and smiled like a ready aunt.

Hannah bore down, squeezed his hand so hard he knew he'd bruise, and pushed. Josh's eyes blurred as he tried to use their bond to take her pain.

Holy shit, how did women do it?

A baby's cry brought him out of his thoughts, and he looked down at his son.

His son.

"You did it," Reed said as he kissed Hannah then Josh.

"A healthy baby boy," North said as he showed off their son then handed him off to Cailin. "Okay, Hannah, one more."

Josh froze. "What?"

"Huh?" Reed said at the same time.

Hannah bit her lip and tried to look innocent. Yeah, not so much. "Um, I didn't want you to worry, but we're having twins."

Josh found his ass on the floor and looked up at Hannah. "Uh..."

"Okay, Dads, get up and help Mom because she needs you," North said, laughter in his tone.

Josh scrambled up as Reed did the same, and held on, and Hannah pushed again.

Twins?

Oh, shit.

After all the trouble of having one, they were having two? What the hell were they going to do with two?

Another baby cried, and Josh blinked.

"A girl," Cailin said, tears running down her face. "Congrats, Momma and Poppas."

Josh moved back to sit on the stool as he watched Cailin clean off both babies while North made sure Hannah was okay.

"Two?" Reed rasped, and Josh nodded.

"Why didn't you tell us?" Josh asked, his voice not quite steady.

"Because I was worried, and I wanted to surprise you," Hannah said as she smiled, her eyes never leaving their babies.

"Well, you surprised us all right."

Josh moved to where Cailin had both babies on the bed, their little bodies pink and wiggling.

He was a dad. Twice over.

Cailin smiled at him and handed one wrapped in a blue blanket. "Your son," she said as Josh carefully held him. He and Reed didn't know which of them was the biological father, but that didn't matter. These babies were *theirs*.

Cailin followed him to Hannah's side, holding his daughter. Hannah held out her hands, and Cailin deftly handed over their girl while Josh very carefully handed Reed their son.

"We'll leave you five alone," North said as he led Cailin out.

Five of them. Two babies.

"Two," Josh said.

"Kaylee and Conner," Hannah said. "Our babies."

Josh leaned down and kissed Kaylee's head. Her little eyes shot open and stared at him, her gaze so focused he knew she knew who he was, even at this young age.

"You're both ours," he said, his voice thick with tears. "Forever."

"Forever," his mates agreed.

Forever.

The End

Next in the Redwood Pack world, Forgiveness, an Adam and Bay novella where the Enforcer shows his heart to the heroine we all know and love.

A Note from Carrie Ann

Thank you so much for reading **BLURRED EXPECTATIONS**. I do hope if you liked this story, that you would please leave a review. Not only does a review spread the word to other readers, they let us authors know if you'd like to see more stories like this from us. I love hearing from readers and talking to them when I can. If you want to make sure you know what's coming next from me, you can sign up for my newsletter at www.CarrieAnnRyan.com; follow me on twitter at @CarrieAnnRyan, or like my Facebook page. I also have a Facebook Fan Club where we have trivia, chats, and other goodies. You guys are the reason I get to do what I do and I thank you.

Make sure you're signed up for my MAILING LIST so you can know when the next releases are available as well as find giveaways and FREE READS.

I love going back and visiting characters. Hannah, Reed, and Josh are some of the most popular characters I've ever written and they mean so much to me! Throughout the Redwood Pack series, you will be able to read more after the HEA novellas, so keep an eye out!

I'm also not leaving this world completely. You've met some of the Talons and because I fell for Gideon the first time he walked on the page to help the Redwoods, I knew I had to tell his story. I also knew I wanted to write some of the Redwood Pack children's stories. Rather than write two full series where I wasn't sure how they would work together, I'm doing one better. The Talon Pack series will be out in early 2015. It is set thirty years in the future and will revolve around the Talon Pack and how they are interacting in the world and with the Redwoods. Because it's set thirty years in the future, I get to write about a few of the Redwood Pack children finding their mates.

The first novel will be about the Talon Alpha Gideon and....Brie, Jasper and Willow's daughter thirty years from now.

If you don't want to wait that long, I also have my Dante's Circle and Montgomery Ink series going in full swing now so there's always a Carrie Ann book on the horizon!

Redwood Pack Series:
Book 1: An Alpha's Path
Book 2: A Taste for a Mate

Want to keep up to date with the
next Carrie Ann Ryan Release?
Receive Text Alerts easily!
Text CARRIE to 24587

About Carrie Ann and her Books

New York Times and USA Today Bestselling Author Carrie Ann Ryan never thought she'd be a writer. Not really. No, she loved math and science and even went on to graduate school in chemistry. Yes, she read as a kid and devoured teen fiction and Harry Potter, but it wasn't until someone handed her a romance book in her late teens that she realized that there was something out there just for her. When another author suggested she use the voices in her head for good and not evil, The Redwood Pack and all her other stories were born.

Carrie Ann is a bestselling author of over twenty novels and novellas and has so much more on her mind (and on her spreadsheets *grins*) that she isn't planning on giving up her dream anytime soon.

www.CarrieAnnRyan.com

Redwood Pack Series:
Book 1: An Alpha's Path
Book 2: A Taste for a Mate
Book 3: Trinity Bound
Book 3.5: A Night Away
Book 4: Enforcer's Redemption
Book 4.5: Blurred Expectations
Book 4.7: Forgiveness
Book 5: Shattered Emotions
Book 6: Hidden Destiny
Book 6.5: A Beta's Haven
Book 7: Fighting Fate
Book 7.5 Loving the Omega
Book 7.7: The Hunted Heart
Book 8: Wicked Wolf

The Talon Pack (Following the Redwood Pack Series):

Book 1: Tattered Loyalties
Book 2: An Alpha's Choice
Book 3: Mated in Mist (Coming in 2016)

The Redwood Pack Volumes:

Redwood Pack Vol 1
Redwood Pack Vol 2
Redwood Pack Vol 3
Redwood Pack Vol 4
Redwood Pack Vol 5
Redwood Pack Vol 6

Montgomery Ink:

Book 0.5: Ink Inspired
Book 0.6: Ink Reunited
Book 1: Delicate Ink
Book 1.5 Forever Ink
Book 2: Tempting Boundaries
Book 3: Harder than Words
Book 4: Written in Ink (Coming Oct 2015)

Book 5: Dreams of Ivory

Tempting Signs Series:
Finally Found You

Excerpt: Forgiveness

From the next novella in New York Times Bestselling Author Carrie Ann Ryan's Redwood Pack Series

She moved with grace, agility, and just that bit of sex appeal that had Adam Jamenson wishing they were alone, naked, sweaty, and doing every dirty thing that came to his mind. If one of the pups around his mate looked at her the way he was, Adam would have to beat the ever-loving crap out of him.

Twice.

Bay Milton—no, Jamenson now, and, boy, did he like the sound of that—planted her feet in the cool grass and fisted her hands at her hips. Her wild, scarlet-red hair blew in the wind in a disarray of curls that reminded Adam of how she looked when she rode him long through the night, her hair bouncing along with those full breasts of hers.

He groaned and shifted his stance, careful not to wake a sleeping, snuggling Micah, who slept strapped into the harness on Adam's chest. Adam knew he must have looked like a completely different person from before, what with his son in a baby harness, the cane he hated using by his side, and his position on the sidelines, rather than in the thick of it.

Things had changed.

He had changed.

At least, he knew he had. He wasn't sure the rest of the Pack knew it yet. They still acted cautious around him, afraid to speak to him harshly or contradict him. That would change with time. He just had to show them that he had, in fact, changed.

"Okay, you guys, you're here because you're ready to find your positions in the Pack, but you don't know how to efficiently control your wolf —yet." Bay strode in front of the line of teens who had long since passed the age of their first change but still lacked the control and discipline needed to be an enforcer in the Redwood Pack.

Not *the* Enforcer. No, that was Adam's job.

One-legged and all.

His mate and love of his life, Bay, had turned out to be one fine Enforcer's mate, doing almost everything he had as the Enforcer, and because of their bond, she felt the same threats to the Pack that he did—just to a lesser extent.

It was as if the goddess knew the Redwoods—and Adam— needed another to step in when Adam was healing.

After all, having one's leg ripped off by a demon wasn't the easiest thing to get over.

If one ever did.

Nevertheless he would heal— he had to.

In fact, he'd already begun to because seeing his mate and child in the hands of the demon, Caym, had stolen any ounce of stubbornness and pride from him. He'd crawled, broken and bleeding, to the depths of any despair he'd thought he'd had and failed.

It had been Bay, his half-demon mate, who'd saved them all.

He watched her move gracefully again, this time

showing the young wolves how to roll to duck a punch. Adam held back a groan as she stood up and wiggled her very sweet ass in snug yoga pants.

He didn't miss the quick glances of some of the older teens either.

Just for fun—and because, hell, he was the Enforcer—he let out a growl, marking what was his.

The young men froze, ducked their heads, and bared their throats. Maybe if he hadn't been sore as hell from standing on his new prosthetic leg for so long, he would have shown those boys exactly whom they were messing with, but he wasn't in the mood.

Plus, he had Micah attached to his chest, and that little one was more important than a pissing contest.

"Adam Jamenson," Bay scolded as she fisted her hands on her hips.

Adam smiled and watched her green eyes narrow and glow gold in annoyance. She was a feisty redhead—but *his* feisty redhead.

"What's wrong, darling?" he said causally, a grin threatening to break out over his face—something that was sure to scare the pups.

He heard a snicker or two from some of the pups who hadn't been watching his mate's ass, but they shut up quickly at her glare.

Then his mate rolled her eyes and tossed her hair behind her shoulders. "I swear boys never grow up, no matter how hard they try."

The girls in the group laughed at that, and Bay joined them.

Adam cleared his throat but didn't tug Bay close like he'd like to. He had to show that they were strong on their own as well as together while they were training. "That's a bit sexist, don't you think?" he teased.

Bay narrowed her eyes a bit more then winked. "Don't get me started on sexism in a werewolf Pack, oh mate of mine. I'll let you off the hook because you happen to be holding the cutest baby in the world."

Micah woke up at his mother's words and gurgled his appreciation. Adam lifted Micah a bit, patted his little diapered butt, and watched as Bay's face brightened. He knew his mate loved their child more than anything in the world, and he didn't fault her for it. No, he loved Micah just as much.

He hadn't always shown it.

He swallowed hard but didn't show any other expression at the memory. God, he'd been such an ass.

A fucking ass.

He'd walked away from his mate when she needed him the most because he'd had to say goodbye to Anna, his first mate who'd died so many years before. He'd walked away emotionally from Bay long before that.

Fuck, he needed to kick his own ass more than Caym had.

Adam was still surprised Bay had even stayed with him. Frankly, he wouldn't have blamed her for picking up Micah and walking away from him without a glance back.

Luckily for him, she'd stayed for Micah and the Pack.

He wasn't sure she'd stayed for him though—not that he deserved it.

He still needed to prove he'd changed. Prove he was worthy of her.

Though he didn't deserve it, he needed her forgiveness.

He watched as Bay finished up the training and sent the pups on their way. Ignoring the pain in his stump, he leaned on his cane to bend down and pick up the yoga mat she'd used to stretch out before the training. Images of just how she'd bent and twisted in order to do so made the pain in his leg worth it.

Because he was a wolf and not a normal human, his recovery time from the forced amputation was abundantly less than what it could have been. Already he could move without his cane if needed, and the prosthesis fit him perfectly. His brother and doctor, North, refitted him every other day. Though Adam knew it was too frequent at this point, he let his brother worry about him only because it not only made Bay feel better but North and their mother as well.

He'd do anything to get the looks of fear off their faces. They'd tried to hide it, but he knew the fear was still there. He knew they were all afraid he'd fall into the abyss again and fracture, turning back into the wolf who drank too much, hurt those he loved, and continually threw his life away. He'd done that before he'd had his anchor—his Bay. And now, with Micah in the picture, he knew he had a future.

That is, as long as they defeated the Centrals.

That was another matter altogether.

"What do you think you're doing?" Bay asked as she took the mat from his hands.

Adam gave a small growl and frowned. "Helping you clean up."

Bay rolled her eyes. "I could have handled it. I don't want you to hurt yourself."

He watched as she winced at her words, but he shook his head before she could apologize. Even though it grated on him, he wasn't about to make an issue of it. He needed her to see him as more than a wounded man, but he also wanted her to need him more. She mattered more.

"I won't push myself. I promise. I just wanted to help my mate." He took her hand in his and brought it to his lips.

Her skin tasted of ice and berries, an intoxicating combination that set his wolf on edge, nudging at his skin. His wolf loved her and her wolf just as much as he did—something he loved about being a werewolf in the first place. There were two of them—two souls—sharing one body that loved and mated the same person and, in Bay's case, who also possessed two wolves.

"She's worth far more than either of us," his wolf said, leaning back to allow Adam the control he needed. It felt good to hear his wolf speak. It had been far too long since they'd shared a relationship where one wasn't afraid of the other—where one didn't blame the other for death and pain.

"Adam, you know I wasn't calling you weak," Bay said as she pulled back, running a hand over Micah's head.

Their son gurgled his delight, and she picked him up out of his harness, nuzzling his soft head against her chin.

Adam ignored her use of the word weak. He wasn't weak, not by a long shot. He was the damn Enforcer of the Redwood Pack—one legged and all.

The sight of his mate holding their child did odd things to Adam. All at once, he wanted to howl to the moon, praising the goddess for his virility as a father, and, at the same time, cover them with his body to ensure their safety.

Apparently, being a father caused one to go 'nucking futs'.

He grinned at the saying of one of the pups he'd taught.

Bay would hurt him if he kept cursing around Micah, and since his son was the smartest son of all sons, he knew Micah would pick up on the words soon.

After all, his Micah was the son of Bay, the most beautiful wolf in the world, and himself—a wolf not too bad if he listened to Bay.

"What is that smile for?" Bay asked as she started walking toward their home, Micah on her hip.

Adam took the mat from her arms and walked beside her, not using his cane as much as he had the previous week. The pain in his stump numbed as he got used to the walk.

"Just thinking about how our child is the smartest and best baby in the world."

Bay let out a laugh that sent shivers down his spine. "You're going to fill his little head with all that nonsense and he'll be one of those babies who pushes other babies around."

She kissed the top of Micah's head after she said it, and Micah let out a small laugh.

Soon their child would start talking and expressing his thoughts. After all, their son was amazing.

"You're doing it again," Bay accused with a laugh in her voice. "You're doing that whole rooster thing where you thrust your chest out and show off your son, proving that your p-e-n-i-s can be wielded like the mightiest of swords."

"He's going to learn to spell that. And p-e-n-i-s isn't a dirty word."

She growled, and Micah let out a yelp. Quickly, she pulled him closer, and Adam took his turn to roll his eyes.

"Really? You're mothering him like he's the best baby in the world."

She glared at him over their son's head.

He winced, not because of her look of "doom", but because of the slight incline in their path. "Only because you're the best mother in the world."

"Don't let your mother hear you say that," she said as they made their way into their home.

He looked over his shoulder, imagining his soft, yet Alpha,

mother coming from behind and attacking him with a wooden spoon—or just her claws. "Don't say that. She could come at any moment."

"Your mother is the one all of us Jamenson women strive to be."

Adam frowned at her tone. "You're an amazing mother, Bay. You don't need to strive to be anyone but who you are."

She turned, rose to her toes, and kissed him softly. "Thank you for that. I was thinking more that if she could deal with the six of you boys and your sister, she can do anything."

Adam threw his head back and laughed. "True. My mother is one he—ck of a mother."

Bay glared at his almost-misstep and continued to the nursery. "I'm going to set him down for his n-a-p, and then we can snuggle." She winked as she said it, and his cock perked up.

Snuggle?

Hell yeah.

He cleared his throat. "I thought it was his dinner time." It wasn't as if he didn't want to snuggle with his mate—dear goddess how he wanted to do that—but they needed to care for Micah first.

Bay lifted a brow and smiled. "I'm going to feed, burp, and change him before his nap. It's the routine."

"Then let me help," Adam put in as he followed her to the nursery. It had once been a tomb of sorrow but now stood as a testament of how much they loved their son.

"When you grow boobs, I'm sure you can," she teased as she sat down in the rocking chair and pulled down her yoga top.

All funny thoughts of him with boobs vanished at the sight of his mate's nipple before Micah attached himself like a greedy glutton.

The sight of his mate feeding their child was another one of those sights that threatened to bring him to his knees. Well, knee, since he had only one, but it was the principle of the matter.

He hobbled forward and leaned down to run a knuckle over the soft slope of her breast above their child's head.

"I love you, oh mate of mine," Bay whispered.

He looked into those green eyes that always ensnared him in the best ways possible. "I love you too." He kissed the top of his son's head then kissed the corner of Bay's mouth. "I'm going to start dinner so you're fed and well before we settle in. While it's cooking, I'll come back and change Micah for you so you can rest."

He needed to do everything he could for her. Words didn't matter. Lies were easily said, easily heard. Actions never lied—even if their intended purpose might be misconstrued.

His Bay had to know he cared for her and needed her in his life. He had to prove he was worth being in hers.

Bay tilted her head and reached out to stroke his cheek. "You don't need to do that. I can handle it."

Adam gave a small smile and pressed her palm to the side of his face, inhaling that sweet scent that brought him home while bringing him to the edge of sanity.

"Let me do this for you."

Let me do everything.

Bay let out a small sigh and jostled Micah. "Of course. I could use the rest."

He knew she was lying, even though she did indeed need to slow down. His Bay was trying to be the Enforcer by his side and learn how to be a new mother, all the while learning what it meant to be part of the Redwood Pack, rather than just a lone wolf.

They had all changed, and if Adam had anything to say about it, it would be for the better.

He walked to the kitchen, ignoring the pain in his stump, and started to make dinner, pulling out the chicken, vegetables, and rice. Though he was a red-meat type of guy—come on, he was a wolf after all—Bay loved eating healthy, so that's what they would do.

She had a sweet tooth he loved to indulge, meaning they went to Willow's Bakery or kitchen whenever they could to get the baked goods that made most want to orgasm on the spot. His brother Jasper, Willow's mate, was a lucky man.

Adam thought about his fierce Bay and smiled. He was pretty lucky as well.

As the chicken was cooking, he leaned against the counter, letting his body rest without the extra weight on his stump. He knew eventually he wouldn't even feel the pain. Though humans would always have to deal with it in some fashion, as a wolf, he would be able to lead a normal life, even if he had to learn to run on a prosthetic leg, so he could protect his family.

As a wolf, he had only three legs, which might have scared some, but he took it as his due. His punishment. He could run with the best of them and fight for his family. Even so, he'd almost felt like he'd never be whole because he'd pushed his family away. It ached at him that he'd hurt them so much but he'd do whatever he could to fix it.

He deserved what he got because he'd hurt Bay so much.

He'd never forget the broken look on her face when he'd walked away—even if he'd only done it to say goodbye to his past. He should have stayed and explained. Instead, he'd broken his mate and almost destroyed their fragile mate bond.

He was the same man who'd beaten Jasper when his brother had threatened to walk away from Willow for her own safety during the beginning stage of their mating. Then, when Adam had thought he'd spend his life alone in penance for letting Anna and their unborn child die, Bay had come into his life, bringing Micah with her.

The grease from chicken popped in the pan, bringing him out of his thoughts. He quickly flipped it over before it burned, letting the smell of garlic and basil fill his nose.

"Micah's down for the count," Bay said as she walked into the kitchen and wrapped her arms around his middle from behind. Her sweet berry-and-ice scent settled over him, and he sighed.

"I thought I was going to do that for you so you could relax."

Bay moved to stand between him and the stove, meeting his eyes. "It was easy for me to do it. You can go in and kiss him later though. I know you love that little boy just as much as I do. You're cooking dinner for us and doing everything else in the house you can these days. Take a breath, Adam. You're going to overwork yourself."

Didn't she see that he had to? Didn't she see that, if he didn't, he'd break because he needed to make sure she knew she and Micah were the best things in his life?

He took the chicken off the burner and turned off the heat before bringing Bay closer. "You're my everything, Bay Jamenson. I'm doing all of this because I can, because I don't want you to have to. You've done so much for me that I can't even breathe because I love you so much. Let me love you."

Bay smiled, her face brightening. "I will always let you do that, dork. You're my everything, just as much as I'm yours. Slow down with me. Okay?" She ran her hands down his back, cupping his ass through his jeans. "What do you say we put the food in the fridge and make out like high school pups?"

Adam threw his head back and laughed. "Soon I'll be able to throw you over my shoulder and carry you to the bedroom. I'll show you just how much of a caveman I still am, but for now, your plan sounds like a great idea."

Bay's eyes darkened at his words, even as the thin rings of gold of her wolf's presence glowed around her irises. "You know what? I'm sure the food will be fine just waiting for us on the counter." She wiggled out of his hold and ran to the bedroom, shucking off her clothes as she did so.

Adam prowled behind her, stripping off his shirt. She'd have to help with his pants and leg, but she liked doing it, and he liked her hands on him.

His wolf growled in appreciation of what was to come, and he smiled.

Oh yes, this was one way to show how much he loved her. His favorite way.

Dust of My Wings

From New York Times Bestselling Author Carrie Ann Ryan's Dante's Circle Series

Humans aren't as alone as they choose to believe. Every human possesses a trait of supernatural that lays dormant within their genetic make-up. Centuries of diluting and breeding have allowed humans to think they are alone and untouched by magic. But what happens when something changes?

Neat freak lab tech, Lily Banner lives her life as any ordinary human. She's dedicated to her work and loves to hang out with her friends at Dante's Circle, their local bar. When she discovers a strange blue dust at work she meets a handsome stranger holding secrets – and maybe her heart. But after a close call with a thunderstorm, she may not be as ordinary as she thinks.

Shade Griffin is a warrior angel sent to Earth to protect the supernaturals' secrets. One problem, he can't stop leaving dust in odd places around town. Now he has to find every ounce of his dust and keep the presence of the supernatural a secret. But after a close encounter with a sexy lab tech and a lightning quick connection, his millennia old loyalties may shift and he could lose more than just his wings in the chaos.

Warning: Contains a sexy angel with a choice to make and a green-eyed lab tech who dreams of a dark-winged stranger. Oh yeah, and a shocking spark that's sure to leave them begging for more.

Ink Inspired

From New York Times Bestselling Author Carrie Ann Ryan's Montgomery Ink Series

Shepard Montgomery loves the feel of a needle in his hands, the ink that he lays on another, and the thrill he gets when his art is finished, appreciated, and loved. At least that's the way it used to be. Now he's struggling to figure out why he's a tattoo artist at all as he wades through the college frat boys and tourists who just want a thrill, not a permanent reminder of their trip. Once he sees the Ice Princess walk through Midnight Ink's doors though, he knows he might just have found the inspiration he needs.

Shea Little has spent her life listening to her family's desires. She went to the best schools, participated in the most proper of social events, and almost married the man her family wanted for her. When she ran from that and found a job she actually likes, she thought she'd rebelled enough. Now though, she wants one more thing—only Shepard stands in the way. She'll not only have to let him learn more about her in order to get inked, but find out what it means to be truly free.